To Sean,
With very best wishes from —
Alice Schertle
(and the gorilla)

THE Gorilla IN THE HALL

ALICE SCHERTLE

PAUL GALDONE
drew the pictures

LOTHROP, LEE & SHEPARD COMPANY
A Division of William Morrow & Company, Inc. • New York

1   2   3   4   5   6   7   8   9   10
Library of Congress Cataloging in Publication Data
Schertle, Alice.
     The gorilla in the hall.
SUMMARY: On his birthday, Jack courageously faces the gorilla
hiding in the hall, discovering that five-year-olds can be scarey too.
[1. Gorillas—Fiction] I. Galdone, Paul. II. Title.
PZ7.S3442Go   [E]   76-28799
ISBN 0-688-41781-7   ISBN 0-688-51781-1 lib. bdg.

To Jenny,
and Katie,
and Johnny

A gorilla was hiding in the hall in Jack's house. Perhaps he had escaped from the zoo, or perhaps from Jack's imagination. In any case, Jack knew he was there. He had been there as long as Jack could remember.

There was a dark, sort of shadowy place next to the grandfather clock. The gorilla liked to hide there.

Jack had never exactly *seen* the gorilla. He just knew he was there. So Jack always ran past the shadowy place as fast as he could.

When Jack was three, his mother said,
"Don't be afraid, dear."

His father said, "There's nothing in the hall,
son."

His big brother said, "What a weirdo!"

When he was four, Jack's mother said,
"Don't be silly, dear."

His father said, "Be a *big boy,* son."

His big brother said, "What a weirdo!"

Jack listened to what they said. He thought
about walking right up to the grandfather
clock. But he decided he would wait until he
was five.

On the night of Jack's fifth birthday, he didn't run past the grandfather clock. Instead, Jack stopped and stared right into the shadows. There was the gorilla, all right. He was big and hairy, and he looked like a troublemaker.

Jack stared at the gorilla. The gorilla stared
at Jack. Neither of them said anything.
Then the gorilla jumped out
and began making
scarey faces at Jack.

When the gorilla was through, he waited for
Jack to be scared.

Jack just frowned.
The gorilla looked
puzzled.
He shuffled his feet.
Finally he asked,
"Are you afraid?"
"No," said Jack.

The gorilla puffed out his hairy chest. He raised his hairy arms over his head. This made him look bigger than ever. He made more faces, scarier than the first ones. When he was finished, he asked, "Are you afraid now?"

"No," said Jack.

The gorilla took a deep breath and made the scariest face of all. To do this he had to cross his eyes and twist his mouth and scrunch his nose and puff out his cheeks so hard that his face felt sore. It was his scariest face by far, but he couldn't hold it very long.

When the gorilla stopped making the face, he was out of breath. He was puffing and panting, but he looked proud. "*Now* are you afraid?" he asked.

"No," said Jack.

The gorilla scratched his hairy head. He looked Jack up and down. Finally he leaned over and stared right into Jack's face.

"You must be just
      a *little* bit afraid,"
            said the gorilla.
                  "Not even a little bit,"
                        said Jack firmly.

The gorilla's shoulders sagged. He sat down on the floor with a *ploomph*. A tear rolled down his hairy cheek. "Why aren't you afraid of me?" he sniffed.

"Because I'm five," said Jack. "And I've decided to stop being afraid of gorillas in the hall." He handed the gorilla a handkerchief. "Blow," he said.

The gorilla blew. He looked at Jack over the top of the handkerchief. "I can growl very loudly," he said. "Then you would surely be afraid. Maybe I will growl *and* make scarey faces!"

"If you do," said Jack, "*I* will scare *you*!"

The gorilla stood up quickly. He began to inch away. "Are five-year-olds scarey?" he asked nervously.

"Very scarey," said Jack.

The gorilla backed away some more.

"I wasn't *really* going to growl," he said.

"Maybe I will scare you anyway," said Jack.

The gorilla tried to hide behind the grand-father clock. Lots of gorilla stuck out on each side. He climbed to the top of the clock and looked down at Jack. "Please don't scare me," he begged. He began to suck his hairy thumb. The grandfather clock began to sway.

The gorilla sucked his thumb harder. The grandfather clock swayed even more.

"Look out!" warned Jack.

But it was too late.

Down fell the gorilla on top of Jack. Down fell the grandfather clock on top of the gorilla.

"Oh, bananas," moaned the gorilla. "Now you will scare me for sure!"

"Maybe I won't," said Jack in a muffled
voice, "if you promise me something. But first
help me get up!"

The gorilla scrambled to his feet. He pushed the grandfather clock carefully back in its place. Then he helped Jack up. "I'll promise anything!" the gorilla said eagerly.

"All right," said Jack. "Promise never to scare anyone again."

"But gorillas are *supposed* to be scarey," said the gorilla. "Besides, I love to make faces."

"Then try this one," said Jack.

So Jack showed the gorilla how to turn up his mouth, and wrinkle his nose, and crinkle his eyes as hard as he could.

The gorilla loved it! "This face feels much better than the other ones!" he said happily.

So the gorilla and Jack shook hands. Then
Jack went on down the hall. And the gorilla
went back home to the zoo,
or to Jack's imagination,
whichever it was.